My Two Families

Story by Michele Gordon
Illustrations by Sharyn Madder

On the first day of the new school year, I was feeling nervous. Some of my friends were in my class, but I didn't know the rest of the children very well. Our teacher, Miss Anderson, had just come to our school. I hoped she would like me.

Miss Anderson asked us what our names were. Then she said, "We will be doing lots of painting and drawing this year because I love teaching art."

I was really pleased about that because I love painting, too.

"I want to get to know you," Miss Anderson said. Then she gave out sheets of paper with squares drawn on them.

"This is a diagram of a family tree," she explained. "I would like you to fill in the names of your parents. If you can, write in the names of your grandparents, too. Get started now. Put your own name down here in the big square at the foot of the page. When you go home tonight, your parents can help you. Fill in as much as you can for homework."

"Homework!" I thought. "Homework on the first day back at school!" I didn't think that was a good idea at all.

When I got home, Mom asked me about my day.

"I think I'm going to like Miss Anderson," I said, "except that she has given us some homework on our first day back!" Then I showed Mom what I had to do.

Mom had a book all about our family. It was really useful. When I had filled in most of the squares on the diagram, Mom looked at it. Then she said, "Alex, don't forget about your other family. Nicky and Tim are your birth parents."

I hadn't forgotten about Nicky and Tim, but I didn't want to tell the whole class about them.

Sometimes I like being adopted. Sometimes I get presents from both my families! But at other times I feel confused because my mom and dad are not my birth parents. Sometimes I wish I wasn't adopted.

I called Tim first. He said he was glad to hear from me. He had a book about his family, too, and he told me what I needed to know.

After that, I called Nicky. She couldn't remember the names of all her grandparents, but she called me back later. She had found out the names of two of them, and she even had some dates.

The next day, when I got to school, I still didn't want to tell everyone in my class about my two families. I didn't want all the children to know that I was adopted. So I decided to talk about my parents, Mom and Dad, and not about Nicky and Tim.

Miss Anderson put everyone's name in a box. When she drew out our names, we had to stand up and talk about our family trees.

It was interesting to hear what the others had to say. Some children had been born in other countries. Some children had grandparents who lived overseas, and who had come to visit them here. One boy could trace his family back to a famous person. "Wow!" we all thought. "That **is** special."

11

A boy named Karl told us he had been born far away in another country. He had lived in an orphanage for most of his life. He told us all he could remember about the orphanage. Every day he had hoped that someone would come and want him to be part of their family.

Miss Anderson said how lucky he was that his parents had chosen him.

I thought so, too. I had two mothers, Mom and Nicky, but for a long time Karl hadn't had a mother at all.

It was my turn next. After hearing Karl's talk, I felt much braver. I decided to show the class both my family trees and to tell everyone I was adopted. I held up my first family tree and told the children about Mom and Dad. I told them about my grandmother, too. She is a well-known painter and some of her paintings are put in art shows.

Then, just as Miss Anderson was about to pull a new name out of the box, I held up my second family tree.

"These are my birth parents," I said. "Their names are Nicky and Tim. I was adopted by Mom and Dad when I was just two weeks old. I see Nicky most holidays and I often call Tim."

The children listened carefully to all the things I told them. When I finished my talk, they all clapped. I felt special, with two families to talk about.

Then Miss Anderson said that she was like me, because she had been adopted, too. That made me feel extra special.

When I got home, I rushed in to tell Mom about my talk. I gave her a big hug.

"Thanks for adopting me," I said. "I love having two families."